Robin Goodfellow and the Giant Dwarf

Robin Goodfellow

McGraw-Hill Book Company

New York   St. Louis   San Francisco
Montreal   Toronto

and the Giant Dwarf

story by Michael Jennings

pictures by Tomie de Paola

For Ike and Etta

Library of Congress Cataloging in Publication Data

Jennings, Michael.
Robin Goodfellow and the giant dwarf.
Summary: A mischievous elf plays a prank on a
slow-witted giant.
[1. Fairies—Fiction. 2. Giants—Fiction]
I. de Paola, Tomie. II. Title.
PZ7.J42987Ro   [E]   81-4860
ISBN 0-07-032451-4   AACR2

1 2 3 4 5 6 7 8 9   R A B P   8 7 6 5 4 3 2 1

MANY PEOPLE are afraid of the Bogeyman. They have heard he is an evil old monster that catches children who misbehave and carries them away.

They are wrong. The Bogeyman's real name is Robin Goodfellow, and there has never been any meanness to his mischief. He's just a frisky elf who likes to play pranks.

One day he came upon a giant sleeping by the side of the road.
Robin tickled him. The giant laughed in his sleep.

The rumble shook the ground so hard that a house down the
road caved in. It didn't matter. It was made of gingerbread, and
the witch who lived there baked another home in no time.

The sleeping giant rolled over on his side. Robin tickled him again. The giant twitched and curled up into a ball. That was just what Robin wanted.

He tied the huge fellow's long, curly beard to his big toes. Robin made very neat bows, then went to hide behind a lollipop tree.

After a while the giant woke up. He yawned and rubbed his eyes as always, but he couldn't stretch as well as usual. When he stood up he was all stooped over. Giants are stronger than they are smart. When he tried to scratch his head he missed, for it wasn't where it used to be. As the puzzled giant hobbled down the road, Robin darted from tree to tree, hiding as he followed.

The giant came to the yard where the Gingerbread Witch was eating the crumbs of her last home. "Did you put a spell on me?" he said.

"Why do you ask?" the witch said, without looking up from her meal.

"I just woke up from my nap," the giant said, "and there's something strange about me."

The witch looked at him, and shrugged. "What's so strange about a big dwarf?"

"That's just it," the giant said. "Before my nap I was a medium-sized giant."

"You must have slept through the earthquake," the witch said wisely. "That's what did it, of course. It could have been worse. You're lucky you weren't made of gingerbread."

"Can you do some magic that will change me back?" the giant asked.

"I could change you into a gingerbread man," the witch said, "but gingerbread men usually get eaten up. I suggest you go home just as you are."

The giant took her advice. On the way home he climbed a hill that had never been there before. He was halfway over it when it snored. Realizing that it was his own big brother, he shook him awake. "Don't sleep here," he said. "If there's an earthquake, bad things will happen to you."

The other giant looked at him oddly, then smiled and patted his head. When his big brother strode off for home, the crouched giant trotted along at his heels.

Their mother met them at the door. "What's that you're bringing in here?" she asked.

The giant's big brother said, "It followed me home, Ma. Can I keep it? I've always wanted a pet gorilla."

When the giant opened his mouth to speak, his mother said, "Why, that's no gorilla. That's a large dwarf."

The giant tried to explain who he really was, but his mother didn't understand. "Go along home now," she insisted, leading him to the door. "If you stay away too long, your own family will worry about you."

The giant trudged through the forest until he came to a small hut. Inside, a group of dwarfs were busy counting the diamonds they had just dug out of their secret mine.

Sticking his head in the door, the giant asked, "Have you been worried about me?"

"We are *now*," the oldest dwarf said, startled. He tried to hide the diamonds under his hat.

"Then my mother was right," the giant said. "It's good to be home at last, Papa."

The worried dwarf didn't listen. "If you must rob us," he sputtered, "please do it quickly and begone! Here, take these and leave us be!"

The dwarf scooped the diamonds into his hat, thrust it into the giant's hands, and slammed the door in his face. The door quivered as the bolt was locked in place. Through the door, the giant heard the dwarf holler at the others, "I told you fellows to be on the lookout for gorillas!"

The giant found a grassy patch in the woods and paced up and down, wondering what to do next. He heard some merry whistling, and then Robin Goodfellow stepped into the clearing.

"Why so downhearted, old chap?" Robin asked cheerfully.

"I want to go home," said the giant, "but I don't know where I belong. Some say I'm a dwarf, others that I'm a gorilla."

"You musn't listen to everyone," Robin said. He sat down on a toadstool. "You're a dwarf. Yessir, definitely a dwarf."

"How can you be so sure?" the giant asked.

"Dwarfs are known for having diamonds," Robin said. "And gorillas don't own hats like that."

"That makes sense," the giant nodded. "You look familiar. Do I know you from somewhere?"

"Possibly," Robin said. "I'm a very famous and handsome prince. Or perhaps we met here in the woods when I was a frog. I used to sit on this very toadstool and go, 'grrrrbbttt, grrrrbbttt'."

"Really?" The giant was very interested. "Until the earthquake, I used to be a giant. How did you become a prince?"

"I got a witch to lift the spell that made me a frog," Robin said.

"I already asked a witch to help me," the giant said, "but she couldn't."

"But you asked the Gingerbread Witch," Robin said. "All she can do is make gingerbread."

The giant cocked his head. "How did *you* know I asked the Gingerbread Witch?"

Robin thought fast. "There are more gingerbread witches than there are any other kind. Being very smart, as well as famous and handsome, I figured it out."

"You *are* smart," the giant said. "Perhaps you can tell me what I should do."

"Why, that's easy," Robin said. "Go to the village and announce a contest. Offer the diamonds as a reward to any witch who can change you back into a giant."

And that's just what the giant did. A crowd gathered in the
village square and watched as witch after witch tried to turn him
back into a giant.

The Ice Cream Witch said some magic words and turned him into a giant banana split, with ten different flavors.

The Candy Witch turned him into a giant chocolate Easter
bunny.

The Soda Pop Witch turned him into a giant fountain that
spouted root beer.

The Frog Prince Witch turned him into a frog and couldn't even turn him into a prince.

But none of them could change him from a dwarf back into a giant. Each blamed the others for ruining her magic. The villagers jeered as all the witches went away muttering threats to get even by casting evil spells on each other.

The giant sat down and cried. Then one last witch pushed through the crowd. "You mustn't give up so easily," the witch said.

"So easily!" the giant sobbed. "They tried everything!"

"Not quite," the witch said. "All they did was say some mumbo-jumbo words."

"What makes you think you can do better?" the giant asked hopelessly.

"Because I am the Earthquake Witch, and I have the magic *touch!*" With that the witch jabbed a finger into the giant's ribs and tickled him. He fell to the ground, rolling around and roaring with laughter. The rumble shook the ground so hard that way off, on the far side of the village, the Gingerbread Witch's house caved in.

The giant twitched so much that the bows in his beard came loose from his toes, and when the witch stopped tickling him he was no longer a dwarf. A mighty cheer rose from the spectators.

The giant stood up to brush himself off. "I don't know how to thank you," he gasped, wiping tears of laughter and joy from his eyes.

"Don't bother," the Earthquake Witch said modestly. "The reward will be thanks enough."

"Oh, yes! I almost forgot," said the giant. He started to stoop for the hatful of diamonds on the ground, to hand it to the witch. Then he thought better of it and straightened. He nudged the hat toward the witch with his foot.

The enthusiastic villagers celebrated the occasion. Two of them hoisted the witch to their shoulders, and two dozen did the same with the giant. Then they marched around chanting what a clever witch was the one, and what a magnificent giant was the other.

When the villagers got tired and left, the giant stuck out his big hand and shook his rescuer in farewell. "Thanks again," he said, and then he loped happily off towards home.

Robin Goodfellow removed his Earthquake Witch disguise and set out through the woods to return the diamonds to their rightful owners. He whistled merrily as he went.

And by the time he reached the dwarfs' hut he had thought of a prank that would be just right for them.

About the Author

MICHAEL JENNINGS has been an advertising man, a newspaperman, a radio broadcaster and a publishing promotion executive. His fiction and nonfiction have appeared in media ranging from comic books to men's magazines. Author of the young-adult, nonfiction title, *Tape Recorder Fun: Be Your Own Favorite Disc Jockey,* his previous books for children are *Mattie Fritts and the Flying Mushroom; Mattie Fritts and the Cuckoo Caper;* and *The Bears Who Came to Breakfix.* Interestingly enough, the bears of that juvenile title also figure prominently in an adult play, *The Briar Patch,* which Mr. Jennings co-authored with Lisa Friedman. Mr. Jennings lives in Rockland County, N. Y. He writes: "An elf of old English folklore is the genesis of our 'Bogeyman.' This book was written to give him a better press."

About the Artist

Award winner TOMIE DE PAOLA is a professional artist, designer, and author of books for children. Many of his works have been listed as Notable Books by the American Library Association, and included as "classroom choices" by the International Reading Association. His *Strega Nona* was a 1976 Caldecott Honor book. Other recent books include *The Clown of God* and *Our Lady of Guadalupe.* Today he lives in a 150-year-old farmhouse in New Hampshire. *Robin Goodfellow and the Giant Dwarf* is one of a hundred plus books that Tomie has illustrated.